Allens Hill Library
3818 County Rd 40
Bloomfield, NY 14469

DEC 2 6 2009

THE BOY WHO RAN
TO THE WOODS

JIM HARRISON

ILLUSTRATED BY TOM POHRT

ATLANTIC MONTHLY PRESS
NEW YORK

Allens Hill Library
3818 County Rd 40
Bloomfield, NY 14469

for Will and John and Georgia—J. H.
for Kara and John—T. P.

Copyright © 2000 by Jim Harrison
Illustrations copyright © 2000 by Tom Pohrt

All rights reserved. No part of this book may be reproduced in any form or by any electronic or mechanical means, including information storage and retrieval systems, without permission in writing from the publisher, except by a reviewer, who may quote brief passages in a review. Any members of educational institutions wishing to photocopy part or all of the work for classroom use, or publishers who would like to obtain permission to include the work in an anthology, should send their inquiries to Grove/Atlantic, Inc., 841 Broadway, New York, NY 10003.

Illustrator's Note: I would like to give special thanks to Jack Kenney and Carrie Klis for their help in the production of this book.

Published simultaneously in Canada
Printed in the United States of America

FIRST EDITION

Library of Congress Cataloging-in-Publication Data
Harrison, Jim, 1937-
   The boy who ran into the woods / by Jim Harrison.
   p. cm.
   Summary: After being blinded in one eye, a young boy becomes wild and unruly, until he discovers the wonders of nature in the Michigan woods near his family's summer cabin.
   ISBN 0-87113-822-0
   [Behavior—Fiction. 2. Nature—Fiction. 3. Self-acceptance—Fiction.] I. Title.

PZ7.H2517 Bo 2000
[Fic]—dc21   00-038056
Smythe-sewn library edition

Atlantic Monthly Press
841 Broadway
New York, NY 10003

00 01 02 03   10 9 8 7 6 5 4 3 2 1

CHAPTER 1

Not really that long ago, fifty years or so, barely a wink and a single tick-tock on earth's ancient clock, a boy lived with his father and mother, and older brother and younger sister, in a small village up in northern Michigan. The town was surrounded by small farms, forests, and lakes, and there was a river running through it, and a millpond that served a lumber mill, and a small factory that made railroad ties out of trees. There was a movie theater that changed features once a week. The theater charged folks only twelve cents for admission so that you could go to the movie and have a butterscotch or chocolate sundae at Bonsall's Drugstore for the total price of a quarter. It was a very good place to be alive.

The hero of our story is named Jimmy and he's seven years old and not particularly heroic. He was a rather ordinary boy and doing quite poorly at school where the only thing he was good at was looking out the window at the school woods where he wanted to be. All Jimmy really liked to do was go fishing, read comic books, enjoy a movie on Saturday afternoon, or ride around the countryside with his father, who was a government employee advising farmers on how to do a better job with their crops, and how to raise better horses, cows, pigs, and chickens. Animals were a wonderful mystery to him and so was the radio. On Sunday evenings his mother cooked hamburgers and the family would sit around the radio and listen to comedy programs that came from far away in New York City. When questioned, his father said New York City was a "thousand miles east of here," and Jimmy followed his finger as it pointed at the east wall of their living room.

The radio also brought frightening news of World War Two, which covered the earth in those days. This was especially upsetting to Jimmy because his two uncles, his father's brothers, had been away at war so long, years in fact, that he wouldn't have been able to remember what they looked like without the photo of them in their sailor suits that stood on the mantel. About once a week the village fire chief, Percy Conrad, would start up the air-raid siren and everyone in town would have to turn out their lights in case the enemy were flying over and wished to bomb their small town. Jimmy's father said this was unlikely indeed as the German and Japanese planes weren't capable of flying all the way across the Atlantic or Pacific Ocean but Jimmy's older brother, John, who was a little crazy, would yell out in the darkness, "I hear the planes coming. Watch out for the bombs!"

One early April Saturday morning the sun was warm when Jimmy ran off to play.

He was angry because the year before he had buried his marbles in a tin box under the porch and now couldn't find the place where he had buried them. This early in April the ground was still frozen under the porch and he couldn't dig very well so he stood in the yard jumping up and down and yelling until his mother came to the door and told him to stop. He continued to yell in anger over his lost frozen marbles, running through a dozen frozen backyards until he reached the woods behind the village hospital. It was there he found his friend Mary Jo, an unhappy girl for reasons no one could figure out. Jim and Mary Jo began quarreling. Mary Jo hit Jimmy in the face with a glass bottle she'd picked up from the hospital junk pile. The glass bottle broke against his face and Mary Jo screamed in fright and ran off toward her home.

Jimmy stood there several moments staring down at his T-shirt, which was becoming

warm and wet and red with blood. His left eye
was blurred and pulsing and began to hurt. He
walked across the street where his friend Dave
lived. David wasn't home but his mother was
and she was a nurse. She called Jimmy's parents,
then picked him up in her arms and ran to
the hospital.

CHAPTER 2

This was the beginning of a difficult time in Jimmy's life. He spent a month in a hospital far away from home in a big city to the south. The doctors operated but couldn't save the sight in his left eye. The doctors patched both eyes so he wouldn't move them and he saw nothing at all for a full week. He had never heard a diesel train at his northern home and when he heard this train's mournful sound from the hospital window he was sure it was a monster coming to devour him, a huge green dragon running in the night toward his hospital room.

It was very upsetting to have both eyes covered for so long, to live in the darkest of darkness as if it were the blackest of nights all of the time. A few beds away in the ward a burned girl cried a lot and the only good sound was the rain on the roof, and his parents' voices when they visited.

The day the bandage was taken off his wounded eye was a terrible shock. He felt he would see only half of the world and would miss the other half. Despite being blind his left eye squinted at the painful sun. The only good thing was that the nurses no longer tied him to the bed at night and he was pleased he could see the brightness of the moon with his blinded eye. The moon meant a great deal to him and he would stand out in the yard a long time to watch it march across the sky.

It took months for the blind eye to heal and by the time he entered the second grade he was sure that all the other boys and girls were staring at him. His father bought him a young dog and Jimmy would hide in the thickets with his dog for days at a time. He became a wild and unruly boy and so did the dog, which soon had to be given to a farmer because it kept tearing people's clothes. Now he felt he had no friends at all and his behavior became worse at school. He refused to learn how to read, and one day at school he even peed on the cloakroom floor, which upset the teacher so much that she beat him, which teachers often did in those days. She used a wood ruler and his ears and head hurt for days.

Things went from bad to worse. His blind eye still hurt but he didn't know how to tell anyone. His brother John, who liked to fib about everything, told him that he should live the life of a wild Indian now that he was injured. So that is what he did. The police

came when Jimmy and a very poor kid
nicknamed Icky, who ate only catsup sandwiches,
dammed up a creek with rocks, causing a flood.
Jimmy ruined his Sunday suit playing in a coal
pile at the lumberyard. Certain other wild boys
began to follow him and one day they all climbed
into the freight car of a train that then began to
move. They were smart enough to jump back out
before it moved too fast, if you can call that
smart. Jimmy led three other boys into an empty,
haunted house, where alone he explored the attic
and basement to challenge the ghosts that lived
there. Without trying too hard Jimmy had
become king of the wild boys, which is not
something to brag about.

By spring things were getting pretty bad and his parents were called to the school to explain why Jimmy had been late nearly every day of the year. His father began to take him on more rides into the country so they could talk things over. His father warned him that if he kept up this behavior he would some day be locked up in a reform school in Lansing for wild boys. One day he helped his father and a farmer pull a calf out of a cow and it was very thrilling, certainly better than school. He held the tiny calf in his arms and kissed its wet face.

The best news of all was that his uncles were coming home from the war, which was finally over. His grandparents had a big party to welcome home their sons from the long years of war and Jimmy got to stay up late, sitting right there between his uncles in their sailor suits until he fell asleep on the sofa. Before he slept he listened to his father and uncles make plans to build a cabin on the shores of a remote lake deep in the forest.

CHAPTER 3

Very early one Saturday in June, just after
school was out for the year, Jimmy was
taken by his father and uncles on a car trip deep
into the forest. This was not like the small woods
near town and when they turned off a gravel
road onto a two-track trail it seemed to him that
they drove miles into the forest until they reached
a deep blue lake bordered with reeds and lily pads.
On the ride Jimmy felt they were driving through
an enchanted dark tunnel and coming out into a
new and beautiful country.

His father and uncles began driving stakes on a hill overlooking the lake so they could figure out just where and how they would build their cabin. His father turned to Jimmy and joked, "You're a wild boy and this is a good place to be wild."

Jimmy didn't know where to start, but when in doubt he always ran as fast as possible, so he began to run. First he ran down the hill toward the lake so fast he ran right into the water up to his knees. Near the shore he jumped over a very large black snake sunning itself and he counted three turtles that tipped themselves off a log in alarm. Not a hundred feet away a great blue heron flapped upward, its wings chuffing against the air. This bird was very large indeed, bigger than himself, so Jimmy changed directions, running back up the hill past his father and uncles and straight into the woods. After a few more minutes he had run so far into the woods that he was quite lost, but then he heard the far-off sound of his father and uncles driving stakes with their hammers so he knew his directions.

It was weeks before Jimmy stopped his
constant running and that was because one day
he became lost for several hours and his father
and uncles were quite upset with him. He was
given a compass and taught how to use it and his
father said he could run only one thousand steps
in any direction. For the first time since his eye
was blinded the year before, Jimmy decided to
obey instructions. Most of the time he kept on
running but his father told him that if he learned
to move quietly, and sometimes sit still in the
forest, he was sure to see more birds and animals.

Jimmy was quite surprised to discover that if he crept around he wouldn't frighten the birds and he was able to sneak quite close to a kingfisher going in and out of its hole in a clay bank. He learned that if he "cawed" the crows cawed back at him. He wore green clothes and watched grouse and woodcock, and one day a bluebird and an indigo bunting stared at each other.

Jimmy found out where the herons lived a mile down the shore and hid in the swamp so he could watch them sit on their nests. On some days he couldn't help himself and chased deer, but then discovered that if he sat very still at dawn beside a creek that emptied into the lake

the deer would come very close to
him. One dawn a bobcat came to
the creek to drink and Jimmy
was pleased that it wasn't as
big as a tiger. Sometimes he'd
walk in the evenings with his uncles.
Both had been wounded in the war and he
felt comfortable with them and wished that he
had lost his eye in the war so everyone would
think he was a hero.

Soon the cabin was finished and his family
moved in for the summer. When they thought he
was asleep in the loft he heard his mother say to
his father that the "wild child," meaning him, was
improving in his behavior. The fact was that he
was too tired from all his running to be very bad.
He also regretted that he had been so busy being
bad he hadn't learned to read and in the fall he
would be in the third grade. His father had given
him some children's Audubon cards but he
couldn't read the names of the birds he had seen
in the woods and on the shore of the lake, or
read the information included on them about

the birds. One rainy morning he asked his mother to help him read about birds and she was pleased to do so. This learning to read was hard work but meant a lot more when he could see the bird he was reading about. His favorite bird was the loon, a gorgeous water bird related to ducks that sang a long clear song that sounded like the crying of ghosts. Like all young people Jimmy liked to be frightened by the mystery of life.

It was the loon that got him in trouble. His brother John was an excellent reader and had read Jimmy many stories about brave Indians and that was what Jimmy wanted to be. Sometimes John made up stories and one dark night he told Jimmy that if he swam past the giant turtles out in the deep water, he could catch the loon that hid out in the reed bed in the middle of the lake.

By this time it was August and very hot and sometimes Jimmy slept outside alone wrapped in a blanket, as he imagined the Indians had done. At first light one morning, after having spent much of the night counting stars, he heard the loon. He slipped into the water and swam strongly toward the reed bed where he thought the loon lived. At any moment he expected immense turtles to pull him underneath and eat him for breakfast but he swam on to the reed bed in the distance. When he was quite close the loon burst from the water, flying away, and Jimmy stood up in the reed bed. He saw a very large snapping turtle but it swam off in the other direction. Suddenly a cool wind blew. It began to rain and Jimmy was a little cold looking off at the cabin on the shore that looked far off indeed. To be honest he felt stupid, but he was a good swimmer. By the time he finally reached shore he resolved to become a little bit smarter. Loons weren't meant to be caught by naked young boys in the middle of the lake at dawn.

Late in August his parents began to pack up
their belongings to move back into town. Jimmy
wanted to run into the woods and cry but his
father guessed that and took him out fishing for a
while in the old wood rowboat. While they fished
his father told him that they would live at the
cabin every summer, where Jimmy could be as
wild as he wished, but that now he had to go back
to school. At school he could remain wild at heart
but he had to learn to behave at least as well as the

average dog. Did Jimmy agree? They shook hands in the old wood rowboat.

Very early on the morning of the first day of school, before his family was awake, Jimmy went into the bathroom and looked at himself in the mirror for the first time in months. He decided that his blind eye didn't look all that bad, just a little funny, and besides, there was nothing to be done about it. He actually wanted to go to school so he could learn about the world he had discovered running through the woods. How did birds fly? Where did they live in winter? How long could the loon stay under water looking for fish? How did Indians hunt? How do fish see in the dark? Were there any bottomless lakes that reached the center of the earth? He wanted to learn everything about the world of forests, lakes, rivers, birds and beasts, and Indians, a world where he felt he belonged. And he did.

Fifty years later, now an old man, Jimmy spends his summers in a cabin beside a river rather than a lake. He remembers his childhood as if it took place yesterday. Life is a flowing river and the river changes but it is still a river. He can feel the child in him when he tracks bears, but not too closely, or when, one early evening, he saw a very large wolf in his driveway, which raised his hair and made his skin prickle.

Often he walks very early in the morning with his dog because that is when the birds loudly call. The natural world seems more mysterious early in the morning and in a favorite place where the river has made a deep gorge he watches as he did as a child,

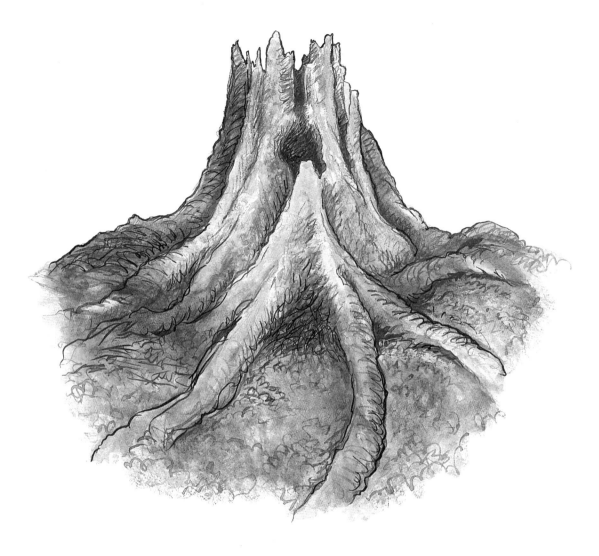

identifying the birds and waiting for animals to
appear. Another favorite place is a vast stump
with roots perched above a gully. You can crawl
under the stump and rest if it's raining. In the
sand under the stump there are tracks of animals
who have found shelter there—skunks, bobcats,
and coyotes.

If you sit a long time in the woods, you are blessed by seeing many things. One morning he sat with his dog for several hours watching a raven funeral. A very old raven fell slowly from branch to branch through a white pine tree. A dozen other ravens in his family flew around and around the tree, sometimes sitting beside him, until he finally died, as we all must someday.

Old Jimmy remembers with a smile the entire story of his difficult childhood. He is sitting on the shore of a huge lake watching a loon sing its lovely, ghostly song far out in the water. A little ways down the shore three curious ravens stand on the sand looking out at the loon. The ravens look at Jimmy, who was at that moment both old and very young, and Jimmy looks at the loon far off in the water singing the song that brings everyone to life.

Allens Hill Library
3818 County Rd 40
Bloomfield, NY 14469